THE FLAME THAT STILL BURNS

(NECROGAMY)

THE FLAME THAT STILL BURNS

(NECROGAMY)

DEVI RAGHUVANSHI

Anecdote
Publishing House

Anecdote
Publishing House

Anecdote Publishing House
E-35-A, E Block, Gali No. 2 Ganesh Nagar,
Pandav Nagar Complex Delhi-110092

Published by Anecdote Publishing House

First Edition 2022

ISBN
978-81-952518-6-5
MRP ₹ 175

Book Promoted and Marketed by Champ Readers Pvt. Ltd.

Edited by Mansi Narula Kashyap
Layout by Graphic Tailor
Printed by Thomson Press (India) Ltd, New Delhi

Dedication

Dedicated to my Parents who made me read and write, while they were just the farmers. This book is also dedicated to the people who have suggested writing a book which could be unique in nature and subject and also to my readers who have made my two books "Mohini, The Tigress" and "Urmila-Unspoken & Unappreciated" the BEST SELLERS. The author is not an authority in Medicines or Medical Science so any mistake or wrong interpretation may kindly be taken as the content of the story.

Acknowledgement

I acknowledge and express my gratitude to my wife SUSHMA, for the input, spell check and all the inspiration and ideas, I conceived watching the degree of her patience.

My elder daughter PREETI deserves special thanks for the content resource, for the emotional and financial support in bringing out the publication of this book.

I would like PAYAL, my younger daughter, to be a partner in this endeavour. Frankly speaking I have copied some of her blogs to make my book rich and true.

I would also express my special thanks to Mr. Rajesh Chaurasia, my colleague, for typing the entire manuscript. Finally I thank all my friends on Facebook, my college mates, for encouraging me to write this book. My heartfelt thanks, will not be complete unless I mention the big help I got from "Bhagvad Gita' and 'Google'. You all are part of my efforts BIG or SMALL.

01

Mahi was the only daughter of Captain Abhimanyu Singh and Anandita Singh. She was the daughter of an army officer and her mother was a Headmistress of a public school. She was born privileged and she was aware of it. She grew up in a safe cantonment amidst greenery and civility. As a child, she had access to beautiful swimming pools, large lawns, tennis courts, skating rinks, canteens and military hospitals. She could go to libraries and attend wonderful parties. In short, she had a childhood that people only dream of.

Every two or three years, she would move to a new city and make new friends. Captain Abhimanyu Singh encouraged Mahi to take part in sports and extracurricular activities.

Mahi had an inherent instinct of being friendly and was always surrounded by children of her age. For vacations, she would go trekking to remote corners of the country because of the privilege her father's profession offered. While the children of her age were playing hide and seek and watching television series, Mahi was exploring activities like tank riding, rifle shooting, paragliding, horse riding and she would be out on the ground watching the Army Day parade.

Growing up, life was also about wondering why her father couldn't take time off from his work to attend his daughter's annual day. She never understood why only her mother would attend her PTA meetings in school. Mahi knew her father was fantastic at tennis but she could never understand why he couldn't spend more than one evening a month teaching her how to be good at tennis.

She used to wonder why only her mother was present to hug her and say "it's okay, we are going to be fine." She used to ask herself where her father was when she was growing up. And why did he leave for work before she left for school and return after she went to bed? Why did he wake up every single day, in snow or hail, to go for his morning run? There were many questions she anxiously wanted the answers to but it took her mother five minutes to distract her from those questions.

But today, she knew better and she had the answers. Mahi was growing up from a child to a teenager. She understood that her father was an Army officer, a passionate and intelligent man who had dedicated the past twenty years of his life to this nation. He had worked on holidays and through the nights. He had served with pride and conviction. Mahi had the opportunity to visit Ladakh. All those dormant tales of men with courage and zest suddenly came to life. Under deep thought she realized that far away from that paradise, there are men sitting with rifles at altitudes of more than 15000 feet at a temperature of -35 degree Celsius, vigilantly monitoring the Indian borders. If there was a lapse in their attention for even a second, they might lose their lives.

Is that what motivated them to get frostbites, celebrate Diwali and their children's birthdays in isolated deserted mountains far away from civilization she thought to herself. Is it the discount in prices of canteen items or discounted medical facilities or glorious salary or anything else? She was wondering why any man with a sound mind would sacrifice everything, his family, comfort of living and risk his life for a nation whose ungrateful people sit back and talk only of the 'privileges'.

Mahi was growing up with these difficult

questions in her young mind and always used to hug her father on first available opportunities. Anandita was the backbone of her life.

Captain Abhimanyu never explained anything to his daughter but watching her father and his colleagues, Mahi got the answer why her father chose to remain in Indian Army, and serve and sacrifice because of the pride he had for his nation. Her father was full of patriotism, the spirit of expectation and commitment. He adorned his uniform and took pride in it. He used to salute the *Tiranga* (flag) and shout *'Jai Hind'* with enthusiasm.

02

Mahi was in 10th standard. She was getting more inquisitive about everything around her. Once a daddy's princess, she was now a teenager who had several questions and was eager to know the answers. For Anandita, it was a phase in her kid's life where her parenting needed to shift gears as her teenager would be exposed to a whole new world full of opportunities as well as pitfalls. Anandita was an inspiration to Mahi. She always used to quote, "The future belongs to those who believe in the beauty of their dreams. You have to be authentic, you have to be true and you have to believe in yourself."

The onset of adolescence brings a dramatic change in the behavior of teenagers like beginning to separate from mother and father and become more independent. However, Mahi, except for some physical growth, was still grounded emotionally and intellectually. She was still her mom's doll, full of innocence and beauty. Anandita was confident about everything happening in her daughter's life but still as a responsible mother and dual role player, as Mahi's father was away doing his patriotic duty, she was watching Mahi growing up rapidly. She was very particular that Mahi shouldn't gain or lose much weight, should be free from sleep disorders, doesn't skip school and maintain her grades. She made sure to keep Mahi away from tobacco, alcohol or drugs.

It was not only Mahi's mother but men, women, young and old in the entire cantonment who used to say that Mahi was stunning, beautiful, smart, educated, well-to-do, yet so friendly, humble and down to earth. They used to say that she was unique because she sounded like she was not living her life to win anyone's approval. She was easy to get along with because she didn't expect anything from anyone, even the compliments. Mahi never used to consider herself superior to others because of her family status and good education. She never behaved like a princess just because of her beautiful appearance. Mahi was genuine and that made her impressive. In all seriousness, she was rare and her upbringing and personality was the result of conscious efforts and hard work of both Anandita and Captain Abhimanyu Singh.

All things are possible for those who believe. Mahi was now the head girl of her school. Three years at Mary Immaculate School gave her the confidence to dream, think differently, and achieve the heights of success. Every moment in Mary Immaculate had marked a day in her life. It had made her a better student, a better citizen and, on the whole, a better person. Mahi thanked all the faculty members as well as her classmates for believing in her. She assured them with a hope that she would live up to their expectations. The moment she was honored with the title of 'Head Girl', she realized that this was the time to pay back and do something for her school, her second home. She was blessed with an array of opportunities and they had become the highlights of her life. Mahi knew that being a head girl was not all about the position or title. It was about the action she would require to create a change. She believed that no matter what anybody says, one should have faith in oneself, stand for what he or she thinks is right and be courageous to think differently. The change begins with you.

She was a role model in school due to her conduct. She was one of the nicest and friendliest people in the school. Everybody loved her. She had the charm and aura about her which was so positive. She was full of life. She was brilliant academically and apart from that, she participated in other activities and was good at most of them. Last but not the least without which her description would remain incomplete, she always had a huge smile on her face.

Mahi's board exams were on her head and she was busy studying hard for the examination. She performed extremely well and as expected, she topped the exam. Abhimanyu Singh was flying in the air on his daughter's achievement. He couldn't resist writing a letter to her.

Mahi, my little angel

I am a proud father sharing my feelings for you with the help of this letter. Although I am not there, I know you must have been emotional and happy after your result. It is a dream of every student to secure good marks. I know you have been studying hard every day and it is a proud moment for me and our whole family that you have topped in your 10th board examination. I know that you must be missing me but I assure you that we will have a grand celebration for your achievement when I return from N.E. Region.

I am thrilled that you have passed your examination with such excellent marks. I would be sending a small token of love from my side shortly. I know it is relatively too early to decide, but I would request you to plan and think about your higher studies and appear in all the entrance examinations.

Now, I want you to celebrate your success with your mom and friends and I am sending all my love, blessings and prayers to you with the help of this letter. Convey my congratulations and gratitude to mom. Lots of good wishes and love for you!

Papa

Tears trickled down from the almond shaped eyes of Mahi after reading her father's letter. Anandita consoled her and hugged her tightly.

03

Mhow (M.P.) was the base of Captain Abhimanyu Singh where Anandita was staying with Mahi at Mhow. Abhimanyu was posted at N.E. frontier. After passing out from Mary Immaculate School, Daly College located at Indore was the automatic choice of Mahi for 11th standard.

The Daly College was the co-educational and day boarding school. It was founded by Sir Henry Daly of the British Indian Army during colonial rule of Britishers, following an English Public School model in 1870. It was established by Resident Governor of the erstwhile presidency to educate the children of royalty, nobility and aristocracy of Central Indian Princely States of Marathas, Rajputs,

Bundelas and Mohammedans. It was one of the oldest co-educational boarding schools in the world. At present, this school has more than 2000 students affiliated to the Central Board of Secondary Education (CBSE).

Mahi opted for English, Physics, Chemistry, Biology and Mathematics in 11th standard with an aim to either become an engineer or a doctor but her ultimate goal was to serve in Indian Army like her illustrious father. Even though Mhow was very close to her new institution, Mahi's parents preferred to make her a hostler and visit her on weekends. The idea was to ensure that Mahi thrives in a new environment and gets proper education. Boarding school is a preliminary institution where the students live together and study in a safe and protected environment.

The news of Mahi having joined Daly College spread like wildfire. She was known as a beauty with brains in the entire campus including the hostel. Many students of her class and her seniors wanted to take a glimpse of her. Some students even started commenting that she was a look alike of Diya Kumari of Jaipur.

Though the school had the kids of high society aristocratic families of India but the society was too conservative than few others like Mahi who had their own specific clan. Mahi was unconventional. She had a good figure, good facial features and excellent skin complexion. Since her parents were reasonably well off and also from Indian Army background, she had a very good dressing sense. She never wore any make-up, not even basic foundation, concealer, lipstick, eyeliner or mascara, except on the days of social functions or special events. She had flawless skin which was constantly envied by other girls who were jealous of her perfection. She was often mocked as a plastic Barbie doll. It wasn't her fault. Her skin was just that way. Many students from the boarding had hung out with her at the swimming pool several times and nobody saw her applying anything to make her skin glow, the way it did.

Mahi dedicated everything about her looks and personality to her mother, Anandita, who was also the prettiest woman in the cantonment. The young army officers used to hover around her just to gain her attention and glance. The entire adjective of Mahi came from her DNA.

Mahi had a sculpted figure which was twine thin. Her waist was tapered and she had a burnished complexion. A pair of arched eyebrows looked down on sweeping eyelashes. Her delicate ears framed a button nose. A set of dazzling angles - her white teeth gleamed as she blew gently on her carmine red fingernails. It was a pleasure to see her flowing moon shadow black hair. She had enticing constellation black eyes over her puffy, heart shaped lips. Her lips looked strawberry sweet. She had a bouncy personality and a sugary voice which everybody either adored or envied. On top of this, she wore vibrant clothes.

Mahi had a hugantic male fan following. Guys from her batch, younger or older, used to frequently approach her but she stuck to her guns. She was the prettiest girl in Daly College and truly a beauty with brains. She was tall, slim, fair with long and luxurious mane of thick hair, always smiling and dressed in sober Indian and Western attire. Whatever she said or did was never enough to prove her intelligence and hard work and her beauty marred everything. After all, she was Mahi Singh, the daughter of Captain Abhimanyu Singh.

04

Mahi's 11th board exams were a few weeks away. As usual, she was engrossed in the syllabus. She was too much into studying to secure good grades and was far away from all sorts of classroom politics. When her final results were out, everyone was shocked to see her grades including Mahi herself. She had done exceedingly well with top ranking. The junior college authorities at Daly College admitted her in 12th Science group from where her actual career was about to take off. Abhimanyu and Anandita felt proud of their daughter's achievement and cautioned her not to be complacent as the line of her future and further studies would be decided only after the performance in 12th standard examination. They suggested Mahi to stay organized and productive throughout her 12th standard.

For a long time Captain Abhimanyu was posted in field and high altitude insurgency areas so he was constrained to keep his family in peace stations. And like many other army officers, Abhimanyu also had to spend more than half of his service living away from his family. His wife Anandita had seen the joy, pride, tears, hardships, separation, skipped heartbeats, uncertainty, and ecstasy. She had experienced her incredible journey of the last two decades along with her only daughter. Mahi, though never expressed, had matured before age, taking everything in her stride, the good, the bad and occasionally, the ugly.

The mother and daughter duo belonged to a special breed. They were extraordinary because they were in love with a soldier. At times, Anandita in temporary depression used to think that a soldier may never return when he goes on a field posting, defending borders including the highest war zone in the Siachen glacier. The army wife remains in the shadows giving her soldier the much needed moral support, taking care of his children and family in his absence, loving him without any conditions and knowing fully well that his first love will always be the nation. But, Anandita always insulated Mahi from reaching deep into her mom's heart.

Life is full of unexpected surprises and the real surprise is when the wish unexpectedly comes true. Captain Abhimanyu came home on a month long leave. Both Anandita and Mahi were excited. It was God's gift to them especially when Mahi also had summer vacation. They felt that they were on top of the world. Mahi gave her father a tight hug and thanked him for whatever special he did for them. They both were full of emotions and found it easy to portray their feelings to the soldier.

The first thing he suggested was to go for a vacation tour to whichever place they wished. Abhimanyu asked his wife and daughter to participate actively in deciding the tourist destination. When deciding on a vacation destination it is important to be laser focused. In the initial planning stages, the amount of choices might be overwhelming. They created a list of places based on where they had always wanted to go and considered the availability of attractions and activities. They were filtering the places based on nature, varied land and sea activities, spas and dining. Availability of flights and hotels was another important aspect.

Mahi suggested a place which should have beaches, arrangement of cruise travel, facility of water sports and a place with some historical importance. The resort should also provide some entertainment. They all agreed in unison that the Andaman & Nicobar Islands is one of India's best travel destinations. It's beautiful, exotic and an absolute paradise for a traveler consisting of mind blowing beaches, secluded islands, caves and corals. There is nothing not to love about this place. It is a perfect amalgamation of nature and adventure.

Two days after finalization they took the morning flight from Indore to Mumbai and spent a day in AOI (Army Officers Institute). Next day, they boarded a GoAir flight from Mumbai to Port Blair. The 8 hours 50 minutes flight was quite tiring. It landed at Veer Savarkar International Airport and upon arrival at Mahindra Resorts, great examples of hospitality were shown. They received a warm welcome from them with *aarti*, *tikka* and garland at the lobby. The welcome drink was quite refreshing. When *tikka* was applied with a fresh flower garland to 5 feet 7 inches tall and pretty girl, Mahi, many people around mistook her to be Manya Singh, Miss India VLC. According to those people, Mahi had a better complexion than many beauty pageants.

Their rooms were cleaned and spacious bathroom amenities that they provided were upto mark. The food at the restaurant was totally value for money. Staff at the restaurant were always on their toes to fulfill their requirements with a smile on their faces.

From the next day, their tour for 8 days and 7 nights started. The first site on day one was Corbyn's cave, a serene beach set in a picturesque background of lush green coconut palms and pleasant sea. Later, they witnessed the light and sound show at Cellular Jail. The show was the saga of countless martyrs of Indian independence struggle who were kept prisoners in Cellular Jail. Mahi revisited the history and after enjoying the first day returned to the resort for an evening stay.

On the second day, after breakfast they planned to visit Ross Island and North Bay Island. They were taken to Jetty in a private car. From there they were carried to Ross Island in a ferry and then to North Bay. North Bay Island is known for colourful corals and marine life. To get the clear view of the island, they went to the glass bottom boat ride, snorkeling or scuba diving. This was the best part for Mahi and after spending about an hour they headed back to the hotel.

On the third day, they took a cab and headed to the Jetty, boarded the cruise to Havelock and enjoyed a 90 minutes trip by sea. After lunch at the hotel, they proceeded to Radha Nagar Beach and enjoyed the gorgeous sunset.

On the fourth day, after waking up to an amazing morning, they planned to spend a day on a water adventure at Elephant Beach. It had crystal clear water and they again enjoyed snorkeling and scuba diving. Next day, they visited Neil Island in a ferry, took some rest and headed for lunch which was followed by sightseeing. Neil is home to three beautiful beaches Sitapur, Laxmanpur and Bharatpur. They were able to enjoy the beauty of Sitapur only and also witnessed some water activities. They also enjoyed the mesmerizing sunset and returned to the hotel for the night stay

Day six was followed by a trip to Laxmanpur and Bharatpur beaches. They had already checked out from the hotel and were lazing around on these two beautiful beaches. They reached Port Blair and checked in the hotel for a comfortable stay.

Seventh day was quite an exciting one. After having a lavish breakfast, they got ready to visit Baratang Island. Beautiful limestone caves and mud volcanoes were present at the Island. Mahi enjoyed it a lot. The route to these caves passed through the tribal reserves and dense forests. Mahi enjoyed this scene the most and returned to Port Blair hotel before the sunset.

On the last day, after a rich and sumptuous breakfast, they checked out of the hotel and took a tour of the city. They visited the Anthropological Museum and Cellular Jail leaving Mahi with a guide while Abhimanyu and Anandita chose to go shopping and picked some souvenirs and antiques. Finally, they headed to the airport and boarded the flight to Indore.

Mahi wanted to pen down her experience and she decided to write a blog about her visit to Andaman and Nicobar Islands. She wrote:

Here are a few reasons to consider Andaman and Nicobar Islands as your next holiday destination and once in a lifetime experience:

1) *The place offers picturesque views and never fails to thrill the travelers seeking adventure, beautiful view of the sun, snorkeling, and scuba diving. It is a perfect amalgamation of nature and adventure.*
2) *It provides in depth knowledge of Indian history. One gets to know the sacrifices of our martyrs in Cellular Jail.*
3) *The vacations are economical and within a reasonable budget.*
4) *The people are friendly. The sea food is really mouthwatering and the shopping is pure entertainment and so much fun.*

05

Mahi had many fond memories of her visit to Andaman and Nicobar Islands. She enjoyed the time with her parents and walking the alleys of various hotels and beaches. Her experience at snorkeling and scuba diving was unforgettable.

The 12th board exams were approaching and the time was running out fast. Mahi lost herself in books and cut her off from everything. Anandita was always standing at her back to provide her mental and emotional support. She spoke less but showed the fiercely independent trait to Mahi. She took total control of her daughter. She was playing the most important role in shaping her daughter's future. In fact, she often went through as much stress and anxiety as her daughter did during her exams. Ideally, she was acting as a facilitator of Mahi by motivating and helping her release exam stress when required. She ensured good communication with her daughter and worked towards removing her fear. She made Mahi understand that exams were important and a milestone in one's life but not the end of the road.

Anandita never compared Mahi with others. She knew that even the most well-intentioned comparison could be disheartening for a student and may demotivate her. Instead, she always appreciated her for what she was best at doing. She knew that pressuring her kid to score high marks could result in mental stress. Anandita had her own busy schedule but she ensured that she dedicated maximum time to regulate Mahi's progress and also ensured that her daughter received maximum support and motivation. She understood the total syllabus of Mahi and created exam strategies. She explained to her how to write during exams, which questions to attempt first and what to avoid to finish the paper on time. Anandita was always present emotionally. She used to discuss the feelings of her daughter and listened to her with empathy. She always supported her daughter's confidence.

Anandita, based on her experience as a teacher, prepared a time table according to the syllabus and ensured that Mahi followed the plan. She also advised Mahi to limit the screen time for phone and television. She took extra care of her diet and sleep as both were very important for her child to stay healthy and focused. She specifically emphasized double checking whatever she had done on her answer sheets and always told Mahi that she wasn't competing with anyone else but her own past performance.

06

"The price of success is hard work, dedication to the job and the determination that whether we win or lose, we have applied the best of ourselves to the task at hand."

This was the sole aim of Mahi backed by her mother. She knew the hard work never fails. Anandita was the driving force. Abhimanyu was not physically present with his daughter. But Mahi always reminded herself of her father's saying that 'keep your dreams alive'. He had taught her that to achieve anything requires faith, belief in oneself, vision, hard work, determination and dedication and these things are possible for those who believe. He had told Mahi that she had all these qualities.

The results of CBSE Class 12 board

examination were declared. Around one million candidates had appeared for this exam. Mahi emerged as the topper of this exam. She had scored full 600 marks out of 600 and fetched 100 percent in CBSE. Mahi couldn't believe it when her mother called her to congratulate her for having topped the exam in the entire country. When her father called her, she started crying and said, "Papa, I missed you all through my 12th standard but I drew strength and determination imagining you doing the hardest duty for the nation. Papa, I am your soldier."

The people were asking for celebration but Mahi had told them that she was preparing for her NEET (National Eligibility cum Entrance Test) exam. After a few weeks, she appeared in the entrance exam. Her result was due next month and she had insisted her father come on vacation so that they would celebrate her achievement.

NEET result was out and as anticipated Mahi had secured a perfect score, 720 out of 720. She became the all India topper. Mahi created history by securing full marks in a national exam. She became the first person from Indore to accomplish such a feat. Mahi wanted to become a Brain Surgeon or Neurosurgeon after pursuing her MBBS from AIIMS, Delhi and for further specialization, she wanted to go to the U.S.

Abhimanyu and Anandita knew no bounds of pride and happiness and agreed to Mahi's request for a grand celebration at General Manekshaw Garden Mhow Cantonment. It was a noted and most sought marriage hall that had continuously been catering to all needs of its customers. For Captain Abhimanyu and Anandita this occasion was like a once in lifetime opportunity to celebrate their only daughter's achievement and it was not less than any major army function. They invited the army brass with their families. Mahi invited all her class friends from Mary Immaculate School and Daly College. The venue was pool side of the Olympic size pool of the cantonment area with fruity cocktails, festive floats and creative pool party ideas for bright colourful decor. They had the kind of get-together that people rave about for years.

The gathering was elite. The guests were all dressed up in their formals. There was an army band playing music of their conventional taste. It was a lavish, elaborate, and impressive party. A lot of money was spent on it. It had the best drinks and a large buffet dinner, both vegetarian and non-vegetarian. Mahi wore a typical Punjabi dress with a multi-colored *dupatta* and colourful *mojaris* (shoes). She was looking gorgeous with light makeup. All eyes, young and old, ladies and gents, were on Mahi.

They stared at her and congratulated her. Some smart young officers even commented that Mahi would be the next Miss World or Miss Universe contestant. Mahi danced with her college friends. Everybody enjoyed the party and blessed the young lady.

07

Mahi got admission in AIIMS (All India Institute of Medicine Science), New Delhi and shifted there. But she had a fear that MBBS was tough and there was problem in remembering difficult medical words. She was away from home and her mom who used to support her in all endeavours. She missed her but she remembered her father's words that unless you don't fall into water, you won't learn how to swim. Soon came a voice from her inner self, 'congratulations and welcome to the medical family! If you are passionate about being a doctor then you don't have to worry about the medical nomenclature or confusing topics or subjects'.

Mahi made up her mind not to worry about the syllabus of medical college. She thought it might be tough, huge and daunting but it was interesting too. She told herself that she was an army brat and ready to face anything that life throws at her.

AIIMS is an autonomous medical university located in New Delhi duly recognized by UGC and Medical Council of India. It is ranked 231 in the world in the year 2020 in category of Life Sciences and Medicine was also ranked 1 in South Asia in 2020 in the category of Life Sciences and Medicine, it also features in the world's best Hospitals in 2020. In national ranking it is ranked 1 among all medical colleges in India. AIIMS New Delhi was the first Indian Centre to perform a successful cardiac transplant in 1994. There are many firsts attached to AIIMS New Delhi. Mahi was proud to be a MBBS student of such unique and well established institute.

AIIMS main Campus is spread mainly into five locations (a) East Campus having OPD Block, Main Hospital Block, Medical College Research Centre, Hostels, Auditorium and Staff Quarters etc. (b) West Campus Consists mainly Staff Quarters and residences (c) JPNA Trauma Centre Consists of Emergency Services etc. (d) Masjid Moth Campus consist of Post Graduate and Resident Doctor's apartments (e)

Ayurvigyan Nagar Campus is too for faculty and staff residential accommodation.

AIIMS Delhi have some of the unique features;

1) Beautiful interaction and relationship between Seniors and Juniors
2) Freedom and ease of the hostel life
3) Opportunities to pursue your interests and hobbies. You can play various sports, take part in quizzes, become a member of AIIMS music band, read books, hold parties, go on vacations etc.
4) A diverse batch with brilliant minds from different parts of the country
5) Lot of exposure and chance to learn from some of the best professors
6) It has library available 24/7
7) The biggest medical fest in Asia which is attended by thousands of people for socio-cultural events, sports, concerts, dance and drama. In fact it is a 7 days of pure ecstasy.

Mahi's first year of medical college started like a roller coaster ride. She was struggling with her books as her professional exams were going to take place in mid August. It all started with the celebration everywhere a medico at last. Gleam of that White Coat, sounded so cool. Yes, it was indeed cool but there was much more to come and it was not all sunshine. Mahi's biggest apprehension was ragging by seniors in college and hostels. But she knew AIIMS had a really strong anti-ragging committee and she had good protection against any bad behavior. Nobody dared to rag her. She was asked her name, hometown, and NEET rank. Her seniors helped her in many ways like selection of books, references, and lectures. Some female seniors even taught her what kind of clothes to wear in different situations.

Mahi didn't had to deal with any patients in the first year. She studied the non-clinical subjects- Anatomy, Physiology, Biochemistry- during her first year. The students at AIIMS never left a chance to enjoy every bit of activities including politics, sports, debate, and exhibitions, cultural functions and tests. Along with intense focus on academics and learning, Mahi's medical college offered a host of extracurricular activities, world class facilities for sports as well as recreation. Such exposure helped the students to achieve standards at par with the best in the world.

Life at AIIMS was lively and interesting for Mahi. The day never ended. Late night snacks, chit chat and volleyball practice at 2 am was almost a routine. Mahi always felt that her hostel was a home away from home.

08

Mahi had never imagined that her life would be so tiring and mundane. She had become a nerd whose life was confined to studies. She was always engrossed in her medical books and references and her sole aim was to secure the first rank in every exam. She didn't care about anything else. Probably all girls of her age were conscious either about their looks or dresses or hair but Mahi wasn't inclined to these things. She found solace in books and she was happy since her parents wanted to see her successful and feel proud of her. All her family members loved her for being a dedicated and studious girl. However, her cousins were jealous of her because their parents used to scold them for having less marks than Mahi.

She was studying in a new institution with new friends and in a new environment. But she was most excited about her new books. Mahi wished for a peaceful environment for her and her lovely books. She got a good room in a hostel and a nice roommate named Karishma. She was from Chandigarh. She was a cute, lovely, quiet girl. Karishma never interrupted Mahi for any kind of gossip. Mahi never made any friend other than Karishma and neither anyone else befriended her.

One fine day Mahi was studying in the class. She was deeply immersed in her books. Suddenly, someone tapped at her desk. She looked up and there was a six feet tall guy with fair cheeks, messy hair, sparkling eyes, wearing black shirt and white jeans, standing in front of her. Mahi's eyes were stuck on his face. She was trying to understand what his moving lips were saying but the effort was in vain. She couldn't hear anything. She was still lost in her books. The tall guy then waved his hand before her eyes. Mahi's hypnotism broke and she came back to the real world.

"Everyone has gone.There is nobody around. May I know for whom you are waiting?"asked the guy.

Mahi didn't answer. Instead, she closed her books quickly, put them in her bag and left.

After that Mahi saw him at her hostel gate for the first time. He was a charming, cute, lovable guy and had a how can you not love me back look on his face. It was from this moment that Mahi began to notice things apart from her books. She started feeling the musical notes in her heart and began laughing on silliest things too. She felt that after meeting that guy, she turned into a new Mahi. She fell in love with that guy from that day. His name was Ravindra Singh and everyone used to call him Ravi. They didn't talk initially but their eyes did the communication. Everyday when Mahi used to leave for college at 8 in the morning, he would stand near the gate of her hostel waiting for her. She was hesitant to respond first but then she gradually let go off her inhibitions. She started smiling at him. The spark in his eyes when he used to look at Mahi meant a world to her. She was now always eager to catch a glimpse of him. Slowly, they came close and started meeting in the evenings too. Mahi used to go closer to him, touch him, feel his soft skin, tickle his ears and ruffle his hair.

Everyone falls in love while remaining with themselves. Love is the most valuable feeling. It teaches you affection, compromise, sharing, rejection and sometimes betrayal too. But the most important lesson which you learn is to know yourself and your decisions. Even a medical student falls in love. Some fall for their mates while others for their work, dedication and determination.

Mahi was not very sure which side of the fence she was sitting on. But for Ravi, Mahi was not only a classmate but a rare combination of angelic beauty and simmering grace. She was also an exceptionally intelligent student. Ravi was one of the most gregarious and jovial members of his class with an impeccably open mind for the outside world. He had a typical TDH (Tall-Dark-Handsome) look. He was also a cricket fanatic and an astute student with remarkable ability to overcome academic challenges. The script of their scintillating love story almost looked picture perfect towards the end of their second year.

One day Mahi was sitting in a campus park. She was deeply absorbed in her books. After a while, Ravi came and asked her to accompany him to witness his cricket match as he was the opening batsman. Mahi didn't pay attention to him as she was trying to memorize her theory lessons. Ravi got irritated with her behaviour and gave an annoying expression.

"Didn't you hear what I said?" he asked in a harsh tone.

"Everyone has a different choice. I like books, not games or sports", Mahi answered politely.

Ravi got angry and he ran away for his cricket match. Mahi also picked up her bag and walked towards her hostel.

Karishma had attended the cricket match. After returning, she told Mahi everything about the match and Ravi's wonderful performance. Mahi didn't seem enthusiastic while listening to her. She told Karishma that she didn't like talking about these things. Karishma was taken aback and was a bit surprised.

"I am not like you. I am a normal girl who finds happiness outside books. And if you aren't interested in listening, it's fine. I will not disturb you", said Karishma.

Next day Ravi sarcastically asked Karishma, "How do you manage with her? Don't you feel bored?"

Karishma gave him a blank look.

He was quite sarcastic but deep down his eyes Mahi noticed a flame of love and she melted after all every human needs love and caring at certain age because of many factors like hormonal changes etc.

Medical students hardly get time to date. Most of their free time is spent either in studying or hanging out with their classmates. They have to be serious all their life and hardly have fun. Their schedule leaves little time to initiate a relationship. And maintaining a relationship is challenging. Mahi and Ravi were no exception.

Life is full of strange and downright contradictions. At many times in our lives, we find ourselves pulled in two completely opposite but equally compelling directions. It seems that two entirely different people reside within us, each mesmerized and held captive by things completely contrary and contradictory. Mahi was passing through the same phase and her turmoil was insurmountable. She became a stereotypical nerd, somewhat socially awkward and didn't care to participate in other activities.

Mahi was the epitome of class. She exuded elegance with every look she served. Her fashion sense was feminine floral and light with an innocent look made more dramatic by her fair skin and dark hair. She always appeared confident. She was a timeless beauty.

Mahi had been keeping a low profile since the last two years but she has the ability to transform before our eyes from casual NERD to alluring, sporting many different combinations of style in spite of being girl next door. She is keeping a low profile due to her medico commitments but when the star in her does resurface, she would showcase her cool androgynous style and would make all the female folks down there envious of her style quotient. Ravindra Singh decided that he is not going against the rules of nature but he was always seeing the light at the end of the tunnel. Nature has created us all. Our looks, our personality, temperament and talents, we have all gotten it from Nature. He decided, Heaven or Hell, Mahi has to be pulled back from her hibernation and brought back to her natural world.

09

Ravi had a busy schedule. He had to participate in the tournament cricket championship of AIIMS. He could not complete his assignments and had to submit them the next day. Karishma told him to concentrate on his match and she will find a way to get his assignments done. Ravi felt happy and thanked Karishma. She asked Mahi to help him out. She told her to give her assignments to Ravi so he could copy and submit by tomorrow.

"But he must complete his work on his own! Why participate in a tournament when he has a lot of work to do?" Mahi told Kasrishma rudely.

Karishma somehow convinced Mahi to help him and she finally agreed. Mahi gave her assignments to Karishma and she handed them over to Ravi.

Next day, Mahi got her assignments back. She checked them for any damage. She quickly went through them and to her surprise she found a handwritten note from Ravi. It was a love letter. Mahi was shocked to see it. She unfolded it and began to read.

Dear Mahi

I never knew the meaning of love till the day I met you. Having you as my sweetheart is like a dream come true.

I get nervous and speechless whenever I think of sharing my feelings in front of you. So I decided to pen them down. I want to let you know that you are my angel, my true companion, my best friend and my soulmate. I want to tell you that I love you till eternity. I am madly in love with your gentle smile, sparkling eyes, your warm touch and essence of the bond we share. I cherish each and every moment I spend with you. You are the most precious thing in my life.

My love for you is something I'll never run out of. We may have changed since we met two years back but we have only grown closer. There are no words to describe the love I feel for you. It's unwavering, tender and boundless. There is nowhere else I would rather go than be by your side with your hand in mine. In a world where so many things can be uncertain, you are the one thing that I will always be certain of. It started with a dream of a life together and the dream only gets better. We have had so many wonderful memories together. I wish to spend my entire life with you.

Sincerely in love,

yours Ravindra Singh Tomar

Mahi read that letter again and again. When she read the first line, her mind was filled with mixed feelings- anxiety, ecstasy, fear, shock. Her palms and feet turned cold. This was the first time she experienced two different body temperatures. Initially she felt angry but she loved the way Ravi expressed his feelings. Mahi appreciated the way he put up his words and how special she was for him. Mahi recalled how they met and slowly became friends. Though there was a distance between them because of books and medical commitments, Ravi knew the sorrows behind her smile and tears behind her amusement. Mahi thought whenever she was sad and trying to hide it with her words, Ravi always discovered. He made her smile like no one else.

Mahi decided to write a reply to Ravi's letter. She took out a piece of paper from her notebook and wrote:

Dear Ravi

I admire the way you share your dreams and wishes with me. I liked it when you encouraged me to participate in the upcoming VLCC Miss India Contest. You and Karishma are insisting on me but due to exams I'm still confused. It's really a tough time for both of us because our medical studies leave no time to feel and express our love to each other. But be assured that my love for you will be more than yesterday. And I cherish our whispers, touch, tickling your ears and caressing your hair. I might not let you hold me in your arms, I might not allow you to lock your fingers with mine. You may call me stupid, duffer, bookish, nerd but these words make me feel deeper in love with you. I wake up with your thoughts and sleep while thinking about you.

Thank you Ravi for being so nice to me!

Yours Mahi

She folded the note and kept it in her diary. It never reached to Ravi. Mahi's feelings remained unexpressed but Ravi understood them through her glittery eyes. Karishma was the sole witness to their entire love saga.

10

Participation in pageants provides the perfect opportunity for some of the most beautiful and young women to fulfill their ambitions and make their independent identity. Beauty contests can be an important focus of national or regional pride. The winner is required to follow a clear programme such as to participate in different social and cultural events, either in the country or abroad, and in international beauty contests including Miss World. Pageants are for empowered women who have a vision of making themselves stronger and better. The focus on empowerment is something, we could focus on more than just the physical beauty of the women who compete. There is still a part of society who thinks that beauty contests have always been a subject of controversy. Some see them as a platform used to demean women by portraying them as sex objects and some see them as actual empowerment of women.

The next contest was due three months from the final MBBS exam of second year. There were advertisements in leading newspapers and magazines. Posters were at display in all the leading clubs and five star hotels. Huge banners were put on the roadside in all cities including Army and Navy clubs.

Ravi wanted Mahi to participate in the Miss India contest. He bought the print out of eligibility requirements of the contest. It read:

1) *The participant should be unmarried.*
2) *Only Indian nationality participants are able to participate and must have valid proof of nationality.*
3) *The contestant's height must be 5 feet 5 inch and above.*
4) *Contestant should have an Indian passport and could be an overseas Indian citizen.*
5) *The contestant's age should be between 18 to 25 years.*
6) *All participants should carry documents such as passport, birth certificate, school leaving certificate, driving license for age and birth proof.*

The participants can apply through the official

site of the show. They should check all terms and conditions of the show before applying. They should also fill all correct and valid details in the application form. After successful filling of the application form, they need to upload the short talent video.

Ravi and Karishma wanted Mahi to participate in the contest. They insisted she fill the form subject to permission from her parents and the college administration. Mahi agreed. She called her mother and informed her that all her friends and classmates were insisting her to participate and they had approached AIIMS administration.

"Mom, I don't think I'm interested in participating. And I don't think that I could reach that stage. Also, there is a risk of losing one year of MBBS due to the procedure involved", said Mahi to Anandita over phone.

"You are right Mahi. I have even been approached by many senior Army officers. They were insisting that I let you participate in the contest. They were saying that you could be our next Miss India or Miss World. Let me talk to your dad first. His decision will be final", replied Anandita.

She called Abhimanyu and informed him that Mahi's friends want her to participate in the beauty contest. She explained the pros and cons of Mahi's participation. She informed that

1) Mahi is beautiful and her participation would add inner belief, confidence, inner charm and beauty skin deep
2) She would add to her understanding of humanity demands of society as beauty Pageants are the means to guide the beauty in a way for the benefit of society. Many beauty Pageants are a part of various Charitable Trusts.
3) She having a perfect educational background, she would add to her beauty with brains.
4) Mahi with that talent would win the hearts of millions.
5) She would garner the inner fire to do something to become the pride of our country.

To most important factor is that participant in Pageant contest unites the entire nation. The disadvantages of participation are too minor to be ignored.

Abhimanyu carefully listened to her wife and granted his consent.

"Until now, Mahi was known as the daughter of Mr. & Mrs. Abhimanyu. I would be happy to be known as Mahi's father once she wins. I am sure she will. She has that power in her", said Abhimanyu proudly.

Anandita called Mahi and happily informed

her that her father had allowed her to participate in the contest. Ravi and Karishma felt joyful upon hearing that.

Mahi filled the form for the contest. She was crowned the first Femina Miss India with a medical background. The entire nation and medical fraternity celebrated her achievement. Her parents rejoiced in Mahi's victory. She was chosen to represent India at the Miss Universe contest after two months that was going to take place in the United States.

Mahi was given extensive training by the organizers of Femina. She was no longer a bookworm but a sincere and hardworking trainee in a Five Star Resort in Mumbai. In between, she was approached for many commercial ads and few roles in films and soap operas but she politely turned down the offers in spite of a lot of finances involved.

Mahi was called for a press conference. She shared the glimpses of the work that goes around to put together a perfect show. Several journalists asked her to describe her winning moment.

"My winning moment was when I saw the joy and pride in my parents' eyes when my name was announced. Winning a national title in itself is a grand achievement. People see the glamour but not the hard work that goes behind it. Many girls dream about this opportunity but not everyone is lucky enough to get it. So, I respect this opportunity and will be keen to learn and explore new things. My parents have stood like a solid rock behind each and every moment of my life", Mahi replied with a smile and grace.

11

Mahi after winning the Miss India title visited AIIMS, her college and hostel. A big reception was organized by the dean of the institute and Mahi was introduced to all the faculty members and students once again. She met all her friends and hostel mates and enjoyed the moments with them. She felt like her old days. Ravi and Karishma felt that Mahi's behaviour and attitude had changed.

While change is imminent, no one should oppose or be afraid of that. As a person gets to experience a new life they become more practical and wiser. People should learn to appreciate the changes in another person if it's a good change. If your girlfriend has changed due to the above reason you should also grow as a person and keep up a pace with her. One should never stop educating oneself, improve the thinking, and learn from books and seminars.

Ravi's thinking towards Mahi was just a misconception. She had not changed a bit for him and Karishma. They were dear to her. She owed part of her achievement to both of them due to sincere efforts made by them. After they met Mahi for sometime, they realised that their thinking was wrong. They both were emotionally satisfied and felt complete with Mahi. There weren't any complaints from either of them.

12

Before Mahi left for her formal and strenuous training in Mumbai, there were a series of parties in the Army Cantonment at Mhow, Indore, followed by multiple press conferences. Fortunately, Captain Abhimnayu Singh was in Mhow with his wife Anandita and his daughter Mahi.

Abhimanyu arranged a lavish party at the pool side of the cantonment area of Mhow. They invited army officials, journalists and notable dignitaries of Indore and Mhow. The party consisted of delicious vegetarian and non-vegetarian food, and a variety of Indian and continental drinks. The Navy band was playing their tunes among the beautifully lit trees and lawns.

Mahi's parents had become legendary in the armed forces party circle for their opulence. The party was extravagant and spectacular with sumptuous food and unlimited drinks for hundreds of people. Mahi's parents had also sponsored a dance trophy for the winner and it was given to the one who made everyone laugh hard. Everyone in the most ridiculous joy said to themselves, "let's melt into this party, let's melt into the beat and sweat until our hearts call for the luxury of bed and the chaos of our intertwined dreams. But before we faced a guest slurring his speech and asking to get another drink, they requested the Press people to talk to Mahi and not ask difficult and uncomfortable questions and they smiled at journalists.

The journalists asked Mahi to describe her journey and areas of interest. She smiled and answered with modesty.

"This victory means a world to me. I have spent many sleepless nights and worked quite hard to reach here. My blood, sweat and tears have amalgamated into courage to pursue my dreams. I believe that education is the strongest weapon one can have. My interests are diverse ranging from reading, music, yoga to dancing. I observe things that usually go unnoticed and this helps me to truly live in the moment. My mom, dad and books are the three influential elements in my life. And, like my father, I will try to be an explorer. He has always chosen to push his boundaries. I admire my mom a lot. She has also pushed her boundaries and made her mark in various areas like music, social work, etc. It is her versatility and strength from which I draw my inspiration".

"I would complete my medical education even if I become Miss Universe. I would share some secrets with you. My mom wanted me to become Miss India and luckily I became that. But my dad wanted me to become a Neurosurgeon. I would not disappoint him. Dad, your daughter will always respect your wishes", said Mahi.

Upon being asked whether she would join films or social media, she impressed everyone and was applauded by all when she answered she will cross the bridge when it comes but before that she would like to add doctor before her name. Everyone, guests and journalists, blessed her and congratulated her.

13

Mahi started preparations to participate in the Miss Universe contest. It is one of the most recognized and publicized beauty contests in the world. The selection is tough and competitive as the participants are the national winners from across the globe.

Mahi reached Hotel Renaissance, Mumbai, as directed by directors of Femina. Primarily, Mahi needed a certain amount of mental training. From mock interviews to paper work studying, it was crucial for her to know about the stuff properly. Mahi was assisted by personal trainers and the best dietitians and nutritionists for pageant preparation. She joined the gym and got the best personal trainer. She established strong will power and motivation. She also set a goal for her body. Swimming and walking were her weakness which she was doing regularly now.

Wardrobe selection was her favourite area of preparation. She was helped by the best dress designers of the country. She was advised by the panel of personality developers not to be afraid to face the judges and walk like a Miss Universe and continue to work on her body language and personality. They told her it will be nerve wrecking to walk in a swimsuit on stage but she has to assume that she was a Miss Universe already and not belonging to a conservative society.

"You would feel more confident about yourself and your body. Learn to walk confidently, play some music and walk according to the tune of the song. Your English language is fine but you could still polish it", said one of the trainers.

Gym and swimming became Mahi's daily routine. She didn't have to starve. She had the best body. Mahi's army and medical background helped her a lot to achieve whatever was needed. Mumbai culture of films, television, and social media further prepared her to face the unseen. Mahi assured the nation that she would carry the flag with grace and raise Indian tricolour on the international stage. She believed this would remind fellow citizens what it means to be an Indian.

"If I am chosen as Miss Universe, the crown won't be the greatest honour of my life, but the pride of our country. India that remains to be my greatest honour and my crowning glory. I would like to be remembered as the queen who serves".

She made her strategy, created a step by step plan and took the first step towards success and turned all her fears into victory.

14

For Mahi, the countdown for the Miss Universe contest had begun. All her travel documents had already been handed over to Las Vegas, USA, by Femina Magazine, the sole sponsor of the event. Mahi's preparations were on peak. She could notice the glow on her skin and a bright luminaire in her spirits. Her self-confidence was reflecting from her experience of winning moments and she was ready to face the new challenges.

One fine morning, when she was on a treadmill, she felt tired which was unusual. She thought it was because of heavy menstrual bleeding and decreased oestrogen levels. The energy levels usually return to normal after a few days as the hormonal levels begin to rise again. Mahi stopped physical training for a few days.

She resumed walking at a moderate speed on a treadmill for a short duration to try to find her optimal walking speed and the reason for her getting tired at the normal pace. She again felt tired and short of breath. She felt that she needed help. She was given the medication by one of the doctors in the Renaissance Panel. He did not find anything unusual. He advised two days of complete bed rest and eating properly to keep body and weight under control.

Since Mahi was herself a medical student she observed her symptoms keenly. Tiredness was the prominent symptom. She was having trouble staying awake during her prime training periods. She contacted the Head of the Medicine Department, AIIMS and explained her problem to him. He termed it as fatigue.

"With fatigue, you might have unexplained, persistent and relapsing exhaustion. It is similar to how you feel when you have the flu or have missed a lot of sleep. You might also have low energy which may arise when you are under significant stress or you are exercising too much or too little or have a poor diet. When these are the causes, you should make simple lifestyle changes which might cause a significant boost in your energy level", he explained.

He prescribed some vitamins to Mahi. She was worried about diet, lack of sleep, stress and depression. On the other hand, the directors and trainers were worried. They were losing patience with each passing day. One of the members suggested sending Miss India runner up for the Miss Universe contest.

15

Mahi's parents were informed about her deteriorating health. They immediately visited the healthcare section of Renaissance hotel and talked to Mahi. She behaved as if nothing had happened. She didn't want to create panic. Abhimanyu suggested to transfer Mahi either to INHS Asvini, the army hospital in Mumbai or AIIMS, New Delhi. The contest was just 48 days away and the organizers were in a dilemma. They were confused whether to wait for Mahi's recovery or let the Miss India runner up participate in the event.

The expertise technical or manpower available in military hospitals is incomparable to anywhere in India. This confidence is not misplaced when the military medical network is seen in the larger context of India, its size, the myriad challenges and the limited nature of health budgeting which is what makes military hospitals even more remarkable for the larger specialized facilities, are par with the most expensive and posh private sector establishments. Other than the various AIIMS Hospitals set up limitedly across India, there is no state run medical service that can match what the military has managed at such a reasonable price.

The doctors at army hospital, INHS Asvini, advised Mahi's parents to wait for a week for Mahi's full recovery. She was put under the best medical care. Mahi and her parents were worried. They were apprehensive about the recovery time and medical facilities. But the army hospital care was committed to provide clear, accurate and honest information to the patient which was safe and effective based on scientific knowledge and best practices.

Mahi was getting the best possible care. Her only worry was recovery time and her possible participation in the Miss Universe contest. Both Abhimanyu and Anandita assured Mahi that she was in the best hands for her medical treatment.

The doctor assigned to Mahi was the top surgeon. He was specially assigned to her for two reasons. Firstly, she was a national asset.

Secondly, she was the daughter of an Indian army soldier. The doctor had developed a vested interest in ensuring that Mahi received comprehensive patient centered care and positive experience. Mahi was a dear patient to all doctors, nurses and healthcare staff.

16

There wasn't any considerable improvement in Mahi's health even after one week. Femina organizers decided to send Miss India runner up Kavita Kant for Miss Universe contest. The message was conveyed to Mahi which affected her physically and emotionally. She was suffering from a high fever and recurring headache. "There is no despair so absolute as that which comes with the first moments of her first great sorrow. The tragedy doesn't come alone. There was sadness in tears."

Her parents visited the hospital to see her and comforted her. Anandita boldly told her that her tears were not a sign of weakness but power.

"They speak more eloquently than a thousand tongues. They are the messengers of overwhelming grief of deep contrition and unspeakable love", said Anandita.

"Some days are bad. You have to experience sadness to know happiness. Every human walks around with a certain kind of sadness. They may not wear it on their sleeves but it is there if you look deep. First accept sadness, realize that without losing, winning isn't possible. Mahi, this isn't the end of the world. You have much more to do in your life", said Abhimanyu.

Abhimanyu and Anandita along with Dr. Raj Kashyap, an expert in Neurosurgery, honestly told Mahi that the treatment may cause some discomfort, pain, or pressure but it would be temporary.

"Mom, dad, I am proud of you both. I am fortunate to be your daughter who lived the life in cantonments, saw the prestigious uniforms day in and day out. Missing this contest is written in my destiny. Maybe Kavita Kant is more lucky than me. For me, it is not important who does it but Indian tricolour should be raised as a symbol of our achievement. I am quite hopeful that Kavita would probably do better than me. Dad, you have spent your days at mountains including Siachen having sub-zero temperatures. How could you imagine your daughter being so weak that she would be shaken by this petty issue? I am absolutely fine", said Mahi in a low voice.

17

Though Mahi presented a strong attitude to her parents, somewhere deep down her heart she felt rejected and hurt. Maybe the luck was not in her favour. But being rejected doesn't mean that one is not liked, valued or felt important. It just means that at some point or situation things didn't work out. Rejection hurts but it is impossible to avoid it altogether. The better we get at dealing with rejection the less it affects us.

Mahi had to cope with it. Though it was difficult, she acknowledged the rejection and accepted it but the problem with her was that she didn't share her feelings of rejection with someone. She kept all her thoughts and feelings to herself. She was feeling pain and emptiness in her heart. She tried her best to stop thinking about what happened but it was impossible for her to get away with it. It hurt her day by day and she was turning pessimistic. Mahi was trying her best to overcome the negativity. She kept reminding herself of the goodness that was still present around her. She knew that this phase was temporary. Gradually, she started shifting to a more peaceful, productive and focused state.

Mahi's health improved considerably. Her parents requested the doctors to discharge her from the hospital. Mahi insisted on going to AIIMS, New Delhi, to resume her studies. Her parents were happy to see her recover and agreed to send her to college.

After a long break Mahi plunged back into the world of books, assignments and exams to pursue the MBBS degree. She was engrossed in the world of Miss India for one year so it was a bit hard for her to get back to her previous routine. She tried to figure out where to start and how to begin. She had absolutely no idea how she was going to study and appear for the exams. She was trying hard to concentrate on her studies but she failed. Her mind was wandering, unable to stick to her books and topics. Mahi felt anxious and frustrated. She tried deep breathing and other techniques but they didn't prove much helpful. She was unable to completely concentrate on the present moment. Ravi and Karishma noticed Mahi's lack of concentration, confidence and positivity. They were worried about her. Ravi advised Mahi to have faith in Lord Krishna and surrender to him completely.

"Mahi, Lord Krishna is a stronghold for the oppressed. He is with us in times of trouble. It is believed that our worries and problems are removed when we seek refuge from the omnipresent. God is our refuge and strength. a very present help in times of trouble we take refuge in his complete surrender to be happier free from suffering and to feel more secure and stable. Taking refuge at the lotus feet of the lord to attain salvation and free from pursuit/ danger or difficulty. Krishna responds to everyone, devotee or non-devotee. Krishna is within everyone's heart. He takes up different roles for different people. Some people want him as supreme master, some want him as a personal friend, some want him to be a son and still some as a lover. Krishna responds to all devotees equally", said Ravi.

Mahi went through something unexpected that prevented her from her normal routine for six weeks. But this period of sickness put her on an absolute hiatus. Afterwards it took her a lot of patience, modifications in the routine and time to feel normal again. It was quite challenging for her. She thought that she could turn her negative situation into a positive one.

Most of us go through difficult and trying times at some point in our life. Time throws us off balancing things that change us and sometimes make us feel as if we are slowing down, losing everything, and something bad happens. But how a person handles such situations makes the difference and that doesn't necessarily mean bucking down and getting disappointed.

The best way for Mahi was to forget about the big picture for sometime and shift her focus to her set goals that she could accomplish. And it was a continuation of her medical course. This was a powerful way of bringing herself back on the track and there were days when she felt strong and motivated enough to work on her goals and concentrate on her aims. Gradually, she found herself exactly where she was earlier, before the contest. Gratitude was one of the things that helped her get through some of the toughest moments. Her parents were first to deserve her gratitude followed by Ravi and Karishma.

18

Slowly Mahi was coming to terms and was adjusting to the environment of college. Ravi and Karishma were like two rocks standing behind her for all her needs and support. Being a medical student was surely challenging. No matter how passionate she was about medicine, she felt quite overwhelmed sometimes due to hard work and several hours of studying. However, regardless of the advantages of being a doctor, she was aware of the fact that achieving a career in medicine was a difficult task. The hope and expectations of her parents were dependent on her. Mahi realised that for becoming a doctor she had to be highly prepared to work in stressful and difficult situations and do her job honestly. She believed there had to be no room for mistakes and excuses, and she needed to be highly committed and willing to work and study hard.

Mahi wished to be a successful doctor and for that she decided to follow certain habits on a daily basis. She made sure to study hard and apply her medical knowledge in real life to achieve good results and get ahead of others. Apart from rigorous book reading, she learned the art of involving herself in social activities like other successful and well-known doctors. She tried to become more compassionate and empathetic. She developed new skills and network with people around her. She believed that the best service was to give back to the community in whatever way she could. She knew her profession could get boring sometimes. Hence, she decided to enjoy every moment whether good or bad. She was ready to face anything in her life. Mahi polished her strengths and took them to a higher level. She worked extra hard to convert her weakness into strengths. To clear her doubts, she religiously followed her mentors and listened to them carefully. She also took out some time to nurture her relationships. She made sure to spend some time with her family and friends. Also, after each productive day she treated herself with love and care by having a good meal, working out at the gym and an evening walk in her campus.

Every evening she met Karishma and Ravi to discuss everything. Ravi knowingly or unknowingly was occupying the inner space in Mahi's life. She felt Ravi was the one she could trust, love, care and live with. Ravi gave enough hints to Mahi to show that he loved her. One day Ravi expressed his love to Mahi. She smiled and sweetly said that she loved him too. They dreamed about each other and spent a lot of time together. They both were falling for each other every day without any fear of losing.

Both Ravi and Mahi explored the city and travelled to several places. They enjoyed each other's company and cherished every moment spent together. They made some best and unforgettable memories.

Mahi's hard work and Ravi's guidance helped her with a good rank in the final exam. She started preparing for the NEET exam to get admission in neurosurgery.

19

Mahi painstakingly prepared for her NEET exam. After three weeks, she appeared in the exam and was eagerly waiting for her result. After one month, the result was declared and she qualified for the exam. She had secured 10th rank and got admission in AIIMS, New Delhi, in Neurosurgery. Her courses included spine module, vascular module, tumour module, trauma module, malformations followed by 100 MCQ discussion by Neurosurgery Faculty on important topics from national and international universities and medical organizations.

Mahi's classes were to begin after twenty days. She suggested Ravi meet her parents at Mhow for a formal introduction. Anandita and Abhimanyu had already met him at Asvini hospital during Mahi's treatment. Mahi's parents were quite impressed with Ravi. Ravi, though a little hesitant and partially scared, agreed to visit Mhow cantonment with Mahi to meet her parents.

Next day, Mahi and Ravi left for Mhow and met Mahi's parents. Anandita was struggling hard to make him feel welcome. There were of course basic courtesies and respect. Ravi, Anandita and Abhimanyu didn't want to be friends right away. They wanted to have a somewhat cordial relationship and in order to be comfortable Mahi's parents asked him some basic information. Abhimanyu shook hands with Ravi and made him feel at home. Ravi felt a bit nervous. Anandita offered him a glass of juice. Gradually, Ravi felt calm and comfortable. Mahi and Anandita prepared a meal together. While Abhimanyu sat with Ravi and had a small conversation.

"Well uncle, I and Mahi are not in a casual relationship. And it's not even infatuation. We have spent a good amount of time together and talked to each other at length. We would like to live the rest of our life together", said Ravi soberly with a glass of juice in his hand.

"Look, Ravi. Every relationship needs to have trust, understanding, respect and equality. One should never hurt, disrespect, or cheat his or her partner and maintain openness and accountability in a relationship. I hope you know that", replied Abhimanyu.

"Of course uncle. Mahi and I have discussed these things frequently. We both are mature enough to understand the sensitivity and other aspects of a relationship. And that's why we have agreed to stay together", said Ravi.

"Sounds good. So, tell me about your family", asked Abhimanyu. Mahi finished preparing the dinner and sat near her father.

"My dad, Karan Singh Tomar, is a senior architect and town planner in Jaipur Development Authority. And my mom, Saroj, is a housewife. My sister is a principal of a local public school and she is married to the District Magistrate, Allahabad. Besides, we also have a small agricultural land near Jaipur", answered Ravi.

"That's nice! We would like to meet them", said Anandita while coming out from the kitchen.

"Sure aunty. They would be pleased to meet you", said Ravi with a smile.

"Mahi is our only daughter and we both love her a lot. She has been brought up with great care and love and I expect the same from you", said Abhimanyu.

"Don't worry uncle. I am a Cardiologist. I

will not let you down. I promise I take good care of your daughter and maintain the sanctity of our relationship", said Ravi in a promising manner.

"Well, let's have dinner now", said Anandita with a sweet smile on her face.

All of them enjoyed the dinner together. Mahi and Ravi were happy. Ravi promised that he would soon visit them along with his parents.

20

Ravi and Mahi went to AIIMS and got involved in their studies. Ravi frequently met Mahi and spent a lot of time together. They talked, laughed, gossiped and discussed their studies and things related to medicine. Mahi felt comfortable in Ravi's company. They both looked forward to meeting each other everyday. Mahi always used to send texts to Ravi soon after he left for his hostel. They used to talk on the phone and chat late at night. They were completely involved in each other's life.

One day, Mahi and Ravi sat in a garden and discussed their work. They looked into each other's eyes and drew closer. Ravi held Mahi's hand and kissed her lips slowly. Mahi smiled and kissed him back.

Their first kiss was magical. Their emotions ran wild. The eye contact between them communicated desire and the intimate experience. The time stood still. They felt like they were frozen in a moment and could sense each other's heartbeat. The kiss was spontaneous. They both felt nervous when they locked their lips but felt pleasure and ecstasy. After that, whenever they thought about their first kiss, their heart raced and butterflies fluttered in their stomach.

Ravi was away for three months for an advanced cardiac surgery training in England. Their long distance relationship was going well. One fine night after returning from U.K, Ravi went to Mahi's hostel since she had not texted him for the past four days.

"Ravi, I don't want you to get too attached to me", said Mahi out of the blue.

Ravi was worried and shocked to see Mahi's different behaviour. She looked distant and Ravi felt that something was wrong with her. He didn't ask her the reason for not texting. He was widely guessing the probable reasons for his girlfriend avoiding him. He decided to leave and went to his hostel.

At the hostel, Ravi wondered about Mahi's strange behaviour. He kept on figuring out the reasons for her changed behaviour but he couldn't reach any concrete conclusion. He thought Mahi might be facing some family issues. But then he decided to talk to Mahi face to face to avoid any misunderstanding. He tried to stop thinking about it and went to sleep.

Next evening, he met Mahi and asked her why she told him not to be too attached to him. Initially, Mahi avoided answering. But Ravi insisted that she answer.

"It's because I don't know what I want in life and what's stored in my destiny. I am not sure if I am ready for this relationship. I do not know if it is the right moment. I am a bit skeptical whether I deserve you. Ravi, I really enjoyed being with you and loved all the moments we have had together. But I'm still unsure", answered Mahi.

Ravi felt broken after hearing these words from Mahi. He couldn't figure out what went wrong in their relationship as they both were quite comfortable with each other. He was surprised to see the shift in Mahi's words and behaviour. She once used to be eager to see and talk to him. Ravi felt hurt and tried to overcome the loss but he couldn't get over it completely. He was absorbed in Mahi's thoughts and he felt hard to move on. Mahi was the best thing that had happened to him and he dreamt of spending his life with her. Ravi was in deep sorrow.

After a few days, Mahi informed her parents

that she no longer wishes to marry Ravi. She didn't provide a satisfactory explanation to them. Anandita and Abhimanyu were surprised at her decision. They both were happy with Ravi and had grown fond of him. The break up news left them sad and startled. However, they respected Mahi's decision and didn't force her to reveal the reason. Mahi knew that it would hurt her parents but it was her ultimate choice and she didn't want to have second thoughts. Mahi never felt that her parents were not with her.

21

Ravi was shattered and broken. He had found the woman of his dreams and was keen to take their relationship to the next level. But Mahi's decision left him in a lurch. He couldn't find any clue for sudden change in Mahi.

On the other hand, Mahi was nervous because she had to provide a concrete reason to her parents for parting her ways with Ravi otherwise they would ask her again some day. She told her parents that both Ravi and her had different thinking and choices which became the reason for their constant arguments and fights. Hence, she decided to part her ways with him. Though Anandita and Abhimanyu wanted her to resolve the issues with Ravi,

Mahi didn't leave any option for reconciliation. As such her parents stopped convincing her.

Ravi desperately wanted his woman back or at least a convincing reason to leave her. For a romance to stand the test of time we need to be committed and willing to work at it but there wasn't any evident reason so he started working on all possible causes that create a rift between relationships.

Communication problems can manifest at any time in a relationship and can occur for any reason. They can be so minor that one may not notice them but if left unchecked can cause irreparable damage to the relationship. Most relationship failure can be traced back to some kind of communication breakdown.

Ravi looked back to the journey of his relationship with Mahi but didn't find any justified reason for their breakup.

Trust and transparency are the most fundamental ingredients for a successful relationship and if they disappear, restoring it can prove difficult. They both respected their relationship and trusted each other. Ravi felt Mahi trusted him but transparency was missing.

Ravi wondered if Mahi was suffering from some external shock which had radically changed the dynamics of their relationship. He thought she might be going through some sickness or health problem that may have caused communication failure. But how would he know if not intimidated by Mahi, he thought. He had to explore that too.

Communication in a relationship that can break down when our existing pattern of behavior and methods of communication get unhealthy or have a toxic effect on the relationship.

Ravi recalled all his conversations and meetings with Mahi to search for himself whether he did constant criticism of Mahi, or carried out any act or attempt to abuse or hurt Mahi. Answers to all such thoughts were no from Ravi. He felt it was a clear case of stone-walling where Mahi refused to open up and at many instances refused to speak to him. It was a deadlock which Ravi had to break but he wasn't getting any response from Mahi despite texting her many times. Even Mahi's parents proved to be of no help as they too were in complete darkness.

Finally, Ravi decided to keep an eye on Mahi and have a close look on her movements, from her hostel to the college.

22

Mahi returned to the hostel after a brainstorming session on brain surgery with minute details. She was physically and mentally tired, which was causing a drop on her physical, emotional and psychological energy level. She did not have the same desire to eat as it used to be. Even an idea of eating food was making her feel nauseous as if she would vomit if she ate. She tried to sleep but she couldn't. As a medico she thought that it either be due to stress, illness or other temporary interruptions to her normal routine. Everyone experiences occasional sleeping problems so how could Mahi tell whether her difficulty was just a minor issue or sign of a more serious sleep disorder. Somehow she passed that terrible night half slept and half woken. She was confused herself whether she was tired more on waking up than when she went to bed. She could not make it to the classes the next day.

Mahi had a classmate and a close friend Saba Khan who stayed in the next room. Even she was not aware of her medical condition. Mahi unlike other friends including men was much better in hiding her problems or not sharing with them even with her close friends for the reasons best known to her. For Saba, Mahi's behavior was weird as it has happened in the past also when she was upset for about a month but she always replied to Saba "No problems, don't worry". Saba thought that Mahi was just private by Nature or she thinks that she can handle her problems all alone. Saba noticed that something wrong and she is not the same Mahi. Something major is going on in her personal life. Saba started encouraging her that she had a great future ahead. Saba was not able to break the ice. Incidentally Ravi was a common friend by virtue of being in the same profession and same institution.

Saba rang her door bell but it remained unanswered. She sent her a text asking her well-being. She texted her three times at different time intervals, may be once now, once in a few hours and once later that night and next day. When Mahi didn't reply within 24 hours, she texted her one more time telling her that she is worried about her. Even this time her text remained unresponded. That was the time when she lost the patience and needed help from some external source. During these moments Ravi was curiously watching her movements every day since last three days, she was not seen anywhere in hostel and in the classroom. Ravi never wanted to appear like a pest by calling and texting Mahi every now and then without any response from her. For Saba, Mahi was irreplaceable but for Ravi Mahi's love was to inspire him to grow into a better version of himself. Mahi's love was mix of emotions, behaviours and beliefs associated with strong feelings of affection, protectiveness, warmth and respect to her. Saba got the room opened by a master key of the hostel warden.

The moment, Saba got the room opened, she found Mahi lying motionless on the bed. The physician was summoned. Mahi was unconscious. The Doctor on duty carried out some simple first aid steps such as checking her vitals for signs of serious injury. Since Mahi was not breathing, the Doctor performed CPR. Mahi was unconscious and her unconsciousness was an unresponsive state. She was looking as if she was sleeping peacefully and was not reacting or responding to outside events such as loud noises or being touched or shaken.

She was shifted to the hospital and was provided proper medical care and she regained consciousness after 24 hours. She was in position to speak. The parents were called and Mahi spoke to them that she was all right. It was a case of serious mental and physical stress due to ensuing examination. "She is all right and they needed not to take any stress". Saba and Ravi were on her bed side in the hospital 24 hour. Both worried and Mahi was not aware of. She did not confide in Doctor also so the Doctor also concluded that she didn't eat properly hence she is throwing up after meals. She is fainting with no explanation. She is refusing to eat and skipping meals. She is actually having an eating disorder which is a mental health condition. He also confirmed that there is nothing serious, she has to eat properly and take rest. She was discharged after two days. Captain Abhimanyu Singh and Anandita Singh wanted to take her home but she refused by telling them that she had terminal exams after two weeks. Hardly four days passed, she lost appetite and started feeling nausiatic. Mahi was a Doctor herself and after consulting a physician online, she concluded that she might be ill again from an infection, autoimmune or other dysfunction. She may also have a neuro or psychological condition impending her. She needed to eat simple bland foods like rice or broth. The Doctor advised her few Vitamins, fiber supplement.

Even after three days there wasn't any significant improvement, she was constantly losing weight, on the other hand she developed headache. She developed persistent pain unlike Migrane. It was hurting her more when she used to get up in the morning. It was accompanied by vomiting or some new type neurological symptoms. She noticed one thing, when she did some exercise or medication or even during coughing, its intensity used to increase. Even to the extent that whenever she used to change sides in sleep, it used to be severe. All the pain killers available with her or in the pharmacy didn't help her to ease out.

The frequency of getting headache was much more than what it used to be and even worse than what it used to be. So far she was under the impression that she had this headache possibly due to skipped meals or lack of sleep.

Ravi after seeing Mahi suffering and her stubborn attitude of not agreeing to be admitted in AIIMS Hospital, called up Cap Abhimanyu Singh and Anandita Singh and told them that the emergency care is desperately needed for Mahi. He was crying on the phone and his cries made Mahi's parents feel disoriented, depressed and distraught. They rushed to Delhi to be with her daughter. There is nothing quite as special as the unique and unbreakable relationship between a parent and their daughter. Anandita since Mahi's childhood wanted what was best for her daughter and Mahi in response looked up to her parents for inspiration and advice. The relationship may shift and change as time goes on but one thing always remains the same, the unconditional love they both had with Mahi.

Mahi's parents admitted her in hospital and asked her why she did not inform them. Mahi started crying with tears rolling on her cheeks and said "Mom, Dad, I cannot afford to see you sad and never in tears plus God's design is such that body heals everything unusual in it." That's the reason, I allowed myself to heal but this guy, Ravi was desperate to bring you here to take care of me.

Before shifting Mahi from her hostel room to AIIMS Hospital, Anandita was able to read the first page of Mahi's diary which read:

RAVI is;

1. A willingness to prioritize another's well-being or happiness above his own.
2. Extreme feeling of attachment, affection and need.
3. Dramatic, sudden feeling of attraction and respect.
4. A feeling emotion of caring, affection and like.
5. A choice to commit to helping, respecting

and caring for other.

6. Some combination of the above emotions.
7. A love and far away from LUST

Even if they separated by distance but not by soul.

23

Mahi's medical conditions, illness were stressful and was disrupting their lives. Worrying or thinking negatively about possible situation was harmful to her parents and was constantly adding to their levels of anxiety or stress and tension was adversely affecting Anandita's health also. Stress and tensions were affecting them physically in many ways including eyes, jaw, neck, shoulders, lower back and was also causing aches and pains such as headache, migraine, backache and muscular pain etc. They were still sure that Mahi's body like any other human being has an amazing ability to repair itself. Meanwhile some dangerous symptoms started appearing in Mahi's health.

1) Persistent headache from severe to very severe in nature.
2) A constant feeling of Nausia or vomiting.
3) An occasional occurrence of Drowsiness.
4) Sleeping problem every now and then.
5) Mahi developed slight problem in ability to walk or perform natural duties.
6) She was having problems sometimes even to recognize some people or recollection of past events.

Since the symptoms looked acute and serious, the treatment appeared to be out of competence of a normal physician and it was felt to bring some specialists on the scene. Dr.K. K. Pruthi, Chief Neurologist, Dr. Anant Bhargava, Chief Psychologist and Dr.Mahendra Agrwal, Chief Psychiatrist of All India Institute of Medical Science was asked to co-ordinate treatment of Mahi. This high powered panel of Doctors was assigned by Dean, AIIMS New Delhi on a specific recommendation of Health Minister and Defence Minister, Govt. of India. Mahi was treated like a VIP patient, being the daughter of an army officer and also being Miss India.

Since Mahi was not 100 percent mentally alert, Dr.Anant Bhargawa, Chief Psychologist and Dr.Mahendra Agrawal, Chief Psychiatrist were requested to join the line of treatment at a later stage. Before Dr.Pruthi wanted to take Mahi for CT Scan or MRI Scan, waited for few days to monitor vitals of Mahi as he suggested to avoid CT Scan and MRI procedure. Dr.Pruthi was keenly observing the symptoms on every two hourly basis and his observations were recorded as under;

Mahi had;

1) Irritability drowsiness, apathy or forgetfulness.
2) Numbness or tingling in the arms or legs.
3) Dizziness
4) Partial loss of vision or hearing
5) Hallucinations, depression or mood swings
6) Personality changes including abnormal and uncharacteristic behavior
7) Changes in intellect or memory problems
8) Uncoordinated movements, unsteadiness of the body
9) Speech difficulties
10) Loss of sense of smell

Dr. Ravi Tomar added his input regarding Mahi's recent behavioral changes which he was noticing by being on her bed side.

1) Mahi was easy to get along but now she gets easily irritated
2) She used to be a go getter but she has become passive
3) She seems to be relaxed and happy one

minute and the next minute she would start an argument for no apparent reason

Dr.Pruthi's diagnosis so far was leading him towards advance tests on Mahi's neuro system as he did not find anything abnormal on the pathological blood tests for almost all vital paramets. Since Mahi was able to converse, Dr.Pruthi asked Dr.Bhargava and Dr.Agrawal to examine her separately. Both the Doctors after talking to Mahi informed Dr.Pruthi that she has to be examined by brain mapping as she seems to be sick not because of an physicians parameters. Their inputs strengthened the line of treatment as analyzed by Dr.K. K. Pruthi.

Dr.Pruthi carried out the CT Scan of the body including brain. The CT Scan took pictures of the inside of the body using X-rays taken from different angles. Dr.Pruthi was looking for a possibility of bleeding and enlargement of the bone in the skull were also to be seen. Nothing abnormal was detected and finally the Doctors advised Magnetic Resonance Imaging (MRI) which used magnetic field to produce detailed images of the body. A foreign body was noticed in Mahi's brain. MRI was used to measure the tumor's size. A special dye called contrast medium was injected in her vein. MRI created more detailed pictures than CT Scan. In addition to this MRI was done for brain from many angles, spinal cord to assess the type of suspected tumor. According to Dr.Pruthi, this might spread in the CNS. The result of neuro-examination done by the neurologist determined the type, location of the tumor in the brain. Few additional tests were carried out to learn more about tumor. In general diagnosis a brain tumor started with Magnetic Resonance Imaging (MRI). Once Dr.Pruthi was able to see the tumor in the brain, the most common way to determine the type of the brain tumor was to look at the results from the sample of tissue after a biopsy or surgery. Dr. K. K. Pruthi explained to Cap Abhimanyu Singh that an immediate surgery of the brain is needed. Till the surgery is carried out the necessary pills as approved by FDA and MCI were given to Mahi. The Doctor suggested to the parents to have a bold face in front of Mahi, but cautioned them and Ravi that Mahi is in critical stage of treatment. She is a Doctor herself so she was to be explained and communicated by me only. Ravi was entrusted with a responsibility to have a close watch on the movements of Mahi.

The diagnosis of life threatening illness led to significant distress reactions in Mahi's parents experiencing clinically significant levels of post-traumatic stress symptoms. These symptoms would have long term adverse impacts on parent mental health, family functioning and adjustment of their ill child. This experience of having Mahi diagnosed with brain tumor was potentially life threatening or debilitating, was highly distressing for the parents. Mahi's sickness had practically drained the family emotionally and financially. They felt absolutely broken when they heard Mahi saying, "WHY ME?".

24

Taking care of a chronically ill child is one of the most draining and difficult tasks a parent can face. The parents have to fulfil all the needs of a child, be it physical, emotional or financial. Such a situation has a prolonged impact on the entire family.

Mahi was already aware about her sickness. She never revealed it to her parents. But the doctors at the hospital informed them about Mahi's condition and told them to act strong. They politely explained the illness and its treatment to Mahi. The doctors told her that she had to undergo a surgery within a week. Mahi could not sleep the whole night. She eagerly waited for dawn. She was trembling with fear and her eyes were filled with tears.

Ravi was constantly observing Mahi's condition. He had requested Anandita and Abhimanyu not to stay at the hospital during night as they too needed to rest and relax. Ravi stayed with Mahi during nights and he made sure to look after her properly.

It was 2 am and Ravi heard Mahi talking in her sleep. It was unusual and he thought it had happened because of the pills Mahi was prescribed. Mahi was speaking continuously in her sleep. But Ravi wasn't able to hear her words properly. She wasn't clearly audible. Ravi was curious and went near her and closely listened to what she was saying.

"We spent so much time together. I don't know what happened. I don't know what will happen to me. Whole world seems to be fading away. We both were happy with each other", whispered Mahi in her sleep.

Ravi felt sad and couldn't stop crying. He had never expected that Mahi would experience such a phase in her life. The news of Mahi suffering from a brain tumor had devastated Ravi. He prayed for Mahi's speedy recovery.

Next day, Ravi told Mahi that she would be alright. He advised her not to lose hope and dream about things she wanted to achieve in her life. He told her to be strong and not give up easily.

When Saba came to know about Mahi's

condition. She immediately visited the hospital to see her friend. Mahi was sleeping and she didn't disturb her. She went to Ravi and told him that she couldn't believe that Mahi was suffering from such a dreadful problem. She told him Mahi never shared that she was experiencing unusual symptoms lately, otherwise she would have been treated on time. Saba felt sad and prayed for Mahi's good health.

Meanwhile Dr. Pruthi along with his team of doctors entered Mahi's room with a CT scan and MRI report. He informed Ravi and Mahi's parents that as per the reports the most common location of the tumor was the base of the skull and the lower portion of spine joining her brain. He informed them that Mahi would be operated on after three days.

Mahi's date of surgery was approaching and her parents were anxious. Ravi tried his best to calm them down. He assured them that Mahi would be fine and safe after the surgery. He advised them to take care of themselves and think about their daughter as their emotions would weaken her.

Abhimanyu loved his daughter a lot and couldn't imagine his life without her. He didn't want to lose his only daughter. Anandita looked at Mahi and caressed her hair. She kissed her forehead and hugged her tightly. She comforted her and told her that she was brave and strong enough to pass through a tough trial. She tried to give her strength and make her comfortable. She told her that this difficult phase of life would be soon over and she would once again start her studies like before. Mahi looked at her mother and gave a weak smile.

Several tests were carried out before the brain surgery including blood tests, ECG, lung and chest tests and doctors informed Mahi's parents that her tests were fine and they would carry out the surgery.

Ravi was unable to see Mahi's condition. He was beside her every day and had spent sleepless nights. Mahi could see the love and care in his eyes. She could see how worried he was just like her parents. Ravi recalled Mahi's words, "Never ignore a person who loves you, cares for you and misses you. Because one day you might wake up and realise you lost the moon while counting the stars". Ravi cried profusely over the uncertainty of Mahi's life and Anandita tried to console him.

Before Mahi's surgery, Abhimanyu went near her daughter and told her, "Life would throw curveballs at many points but it depends on a person whether to face them or not. Life isn't supposed to be entirely pleasant. It is never like a fairytale. It always tests us and we need to fight back with our head up. And giving up on life is never an option. Success comes to those who after falling in life get up and move ahead. There is always some purpose in our life and we should find it and work on it. Mahi, don't lose hope. We know you are strong just like your father. I am with you always".

He told her to stay strong as life will always test her and she needs to fight back and not give up. Mahi listened to her father carefully and gave him a smile.

"As long as you are alive, you have no excuse to say you can't. So many of our dreams first seem impossible, then they seem improbable and then we summon the will they soon become inevitable. Learn to believe in your dreams and appreciate that you have everything you need. You are strong and nothing can stop the man with the right mental attribute from achieving his goal. It is always dark before dawn".

There was a smile on Mahi's face and a ray of confidence on Ravi and Anandita's face.

25

It was the day of Mahi's surgery. The hardest day of their lives. Mahi was a champion. She was all smiles throughout the pre operation process. Anandita looked calm and composed. Ravi was apprehensive. He didn't know what to say or do. He was struggling with intense and painful emotions. He felt weak and dejected. He recalled Mahi's words, "I don't want you to be too attached to me" and thought now he understood why Mahi said that. His eyes were filled with tears and he prayed for Mahi's well-being.

Mahi was shifted to the operation theatre in the afternoon. Dr. Pruthi with his team of doctors entered the theatre. Mahi looked at them. She saw them in uniform and masks and asked "Are you all going to fix my brain?"

They gave her a smile and nodded. Mahi was given anaesthesia and she quickly fell unconscious. She was in the operation theatre for eight hours. Mahi's parents, Ravi and Saba, were updated every two hours by the nurse named Jennifer. She was humble, supportive and hopeful. She gave them the assurance that Mahi was under safe hands and responding well. In the evening, Dr. Pruthi came out after the successful operation and spoke to them. He told them that the entire tumor was removed and was confident that the doctor on ICU duty would not need a shunt to drain the ventricle. Mahi was shifted to Intensive Care Unit (ICU) soon after the surgery.

26

Mahi was kept in the Neuro Critical Care Unit (NCCU) for five days as against a normal stay of two days to provide extra care in the recovery process. A team of trained doctors and nurses were entrusted with the responsibility to take care of Mahi. Dr. Pruthi explained everything to the doctors and nurses and told them to closely monitor Mahi's condition.

Mahi was able to meet her family and Ravi after six hours but brain surgery was causing some minor problems in her thoughts and behavior. Mahi required help and was taken to rehabilitation specialists such as physical therapist, occupational therapist and speech language of AIIMS. The physical therapists assessed Mahi's ability to walk safely and climb stairs. Her recovery was found to be satisfactory. They were later joined by occupational therapists to assess Mahi's ability of getting dressed, using the toilet and getting in and out of shower. They also tested her vision and thinking skills to determine whether Mahi could return to her classes. She was performing well and the doctors were happy to see her progress. The speech language therapists certified that Mahi's speech was all right and she did not have any swallowing disorders.

After two weeks, she was discharged from the hospital. The doctors advised her parents to contact them immediately if Mahi's faced breathing problems or seizure. Ravi was also advised to keenly monitor all the parameters. Fortunately, Mahi was getting better and responded well. The overall recovery was good but her parents were very careful of her movements.

Anandita carefully washed Mahi's hair after a few days. She gently applied shampoo to her hair and made sure not to touch the incision area. She was taking great care of Mahi.

Six months passed. One day, Ravi visited Mahi's home in the evening. He saw Mahi and told her that she was looking cute and healthy. Mahi gave him a smile which filled Ravi's heart with joy.

After traumatic surgery many couples find that their relationship with each other changes dramatically. These changes are very personal and can be very emotional for both the people in the relationship. The relationship of Mahi and Ravi even became deeper than it used to be earlier. Mahi was a little better and was in a position to move out of the house with an escort.

It was Mahi's birthday the next day. Ravi asked Mahi's parents to allow them for a dinner date. They happily agreed but were a bit skeptical because of Mahi's health. Ravi told them it was healthy for Mahi to go out and she will feel nice. He took her to the best restaurant and made her feel like the most important person in the world.

They sat on the corner table. Ravi ordered hazelnut shake and chocolate waffles. He smiled at Mahi. She was feeling comfortable and liked the peaceful atmosphere. After some time, he kept a gift on the table. Mahi was surprised. Ravi told her to unwrap it. Mahi opened the box and found a book and some chocolates in it. She looked at Ravi with a big smile. She took out the book and read its title. It was a book by Henry Marsh titled as *Admission: A Life in Brain Surgery.* Mahi felt happy and thanked Ravi. She liked the present and Ravi's company. Ravi asked Mahi if she would like to watch a movie with him. But she was feeling tired and politely declined the request. Ravi didn't insist further and happily dropped Mahi to her home.

27

Everything was going well in Mahi's life. She had resumed her Master's classes in AIIMS, New Delhi, after losing one semester. She had plans to complete her studies. She set her agenda and carefully charted her plans and goals. She was confident and determined to complete her course and become a successful neurologist. She promised to herself that she would not let her goals and resolutions fall apart because of her surgery and health condition. She was willing to work hard and pass her exams with great scores. She didn't let negative thoughts overpower her mind. She felt grateful that her painful days made her stronger and she was ready to face any challenge in her life.

She prepared her study schedule and

followed it religiously. Her aim was to top the exam and become a famous doctor. She began to study hard and thoroughly reviewed her progress. She read a lot of medical books and watched tutorial videos on the internet. She appeared in various online quizzes and mock tests to refine her weak areas. She was back to her previous form and was hopeful that she would fulfill her dream.

Mahi used to frequently visit the hospital for check ups along with her parents. Ravi used to also accompany them. The doctors advised her parents to take great precautions and keep Mahi away from any stress. They also told them to continue giving her medicines.

Anandita and Abhimanyu were happy to see Mahi's improvement. Both of them wanted to wed off their daughter as Mahi had reached the right age. They wanted to see Mahi's family. They knew Ravi was the right match for Mahi and Mahi also liked him. Besides, Ravi being a doctor would take good care of her. They decided to meet both of them and discuss their marriage. Anandita called Mahi and Ravi and told them to visit the Mhow cantonment for a small conversation.

Next day, Mahi and Ravi reached Mhow. They were curious to know the reason for the meeting. Before entering the house, they visited the cantonment cafeteria.

Mahi told Ravi that;

Mahi You are a lover when you realize and appreciate the gift that your partner is and you will celebrate that gift every day. You are a lover when you realize that nothing that happened between us will be insignificant and everything you say in the relationship has the potential to cause your beloved joy or sorrow and everything you do will either strengthen your connection or weaken it. You are a lover when you understand all this and wake up each morning filled with gratitude that you have another day to love your partner and enjoy every moment with your partner.

Ravi I strongly believe it, I don't know how to explain the love I feel towards you Mahi.

Mahi Are you kidding? I was impressed and gave him a strange look.

Ravi Never again and kissed her.

Anandita and Abhimanyu told them that they were perfect for each other and should get married after six months and Mahi would continue her studies. They told Mahi that Ravi was a nice guy and he would look after her with great love and care. Mahi smiled and Ravi felt happy and thanked them.

28

Mahi was happy to get married to Ravi. She often thought of him and smiled to herself. She knew she had fallen in love with him but felt shy to openly confess it to Ravi. She found herself thinking about him while sleeping. She recalled the days when she was admitted in the hospital and how Ravi took care of her. She felt grateful and desired to spend her life with him.

Mahi was no longer a book nerd. This time she made sure to give equal time to her studies and Ravi. She was in love and made sure to look great in front of Ravi. Infact, she wanted to spend more time with Ravi. Apart from her studies, she watched movies and listened to some fine music. She also ordered some nice dresses to wear whenever she would get a chance to go out with Ravi. She was feeling better and Ravi's thoughts filled her heart with joy.

Ravi took Mahi on a number of dates. They shared their thoughts and feelings with each other. Ravi also accompanied Mahi to the hospital for her routine check up. Doctors told him that Mahi's health was improving and she was responding well to the medicines. Her appetite was getting better and her body was improving physically. Mahi was happy and felt that Ravi was the reason for her significant improvement.

One day in the evening, after returning from her tiring classes to the hostel, Mahi decided to take a hot shower. She felt calm and relaxed and played some music on her phone. After a while, she coughed continuously which led to shortness of breath. She quickly grabbed a glass of water to calm herself. After a few minutes, she again started coughing and experienced a mild headache and nausea. She was worried and immediately called Ravi.

Ravi took her to the hospital at midnight. He contacted Dr.Pruthi who prescribed some lifesaving drugs to calm down Mahi's disturbing symptoms. Dr. Pruthi advised his team to be present at 9 am at his consulting office along with Mahi's old medical reports. Meanwhile, Mahi began experiencing several symptoms like headache, seizures, memory loss, depression, mood swings, fatigue and some more symptoms exactly similar to the last ones.

Ravi called Mahi's parents and they immediately visited the hospital. They consulted the doctors and asked them the reason for the recurrence of symptoms. Doctors told them that they need to carry out a few tests. Dr. Pruthi said that brain tumors could recur and regrow after the treatment but in Mahi's case surgery was carried out carefully with proper treatment afterwards.

After Mahi's tests report were ready, the doctors concluded that part of the tumor was still present in her brain which had caused further damage. They said it could only be removed surgically since it was spreading in her body. Mahi required immediate surgery. She was taken to the operation theatre. Mahi was anxious and looked at her parents and Ravi with a sad expression. She hugged Anandita and Abhimanyu tightly with tears in her eyes. Ravi assured her that she would be alright. The door of the theatre was locked and Mahi was inside in the hands of doctors.

Anandita and Abhimanyu were worried. They prayed for Mahi's successful operation. Ravi was feeling helpless and walked restlessly outside the theatre. He knew that it was a difficult operation. After an hour, a nurse came out from the theatre and updated them about Mahi's condition. She told them the doctors were still performing the surgery.

Mahi was surrounded by a multidisciplinary team consisting of surgeons, physicians, nurses, pharmacists, counselors, dietitians and rehabilitation specialists. Dr. Pruthi carried out the surgery. There was some viable tumor remaining and after surgery, radiation therapy and chemotherapy was proposed. Successfully treating a brain tumor was challenging for them. Mahi was injected with corticosteroids to lower the swelling in the brain. She was also injected with anti-seizure medicine to control the seizures. After five hours, the surgery was over and she was shifted to ICU.

In the ICU, Mahi suffered sudden bouts of convulsions and was moving towards coma. The doctors tried their best to help Mahi get out of the coma. Mahi experienced a stroke and a blood clot blocked the blood supply to part of her brain. Her brain was completely damaged. The doctors tried all means to revive her life. They did their best but the final cardiac arrest took away Mahi's life.

Dr. Pruthi came out of the ICU and with a sad expression informed Anandita, Abhimanyu and Ravi that Mahi was no more. They failed to save her.

29

The death of a young child comes as a great shock for parents. It is a difficult and painful experience that shatters them physically and emotionally. It becomes tough for them to endure this lifelong pain.

Both Anandita and Abhimanyu were crippled. They were in tears and unable to console each other. They couldn't believe their only daughter was no longer with them. Ravi was in deep shock. The girl whom he loved so deeply left her forever. The cheerful face of Mahi flashed in front of his eyes. His heart sank and he felt dejected.

Mahi's body was draped in a white cloth and taken to her home in an ambulance. It was kept in a drawing room. Anandita, Abhimanyu and

Ravi sat there in silence. The moments spent with Mahi flashed in front of them. Anandita was crying silently. Abhimanyu stared at a small doll kept in a corner of a shelf. He was taken back to Mahi's childhood and the day when he purchased that doll for Mahi while returning from his duty. He could see the smiling face of little Mahi near the doll and hear her giggles and laughter. He remembered the upset face of Mahi when her dad left for his duty after the vacation. He then looked at Mahi's motionless body and tears rolled down his face slowly. He wanted to see her as a successful doctor. He had dreamed of her wedding. But now all his wishes and dreams were broken and he felt helpless.

Anandita recalled the day when she held baby Mahi in her arms for the first time. Her innocent and beautiful face had filled her heart with infinite joy that time. She remembered that special day when Mahi called her 'mom' and she felt on the top of the world. She recollected the memories of Mahi's school days, her sweet voice, smile and laughter. She cried endlessly.

Ravi wiped his tears, cleared his throat and after a long silence he turned towards Anandita and Abhimanyu.

"Uncle, aunty, Mahi left us suddenly and I wasn't able to tell her how much I loved her. I didn't get a chance to express my love to her in a proper way and bid her a memorable goodbye.

Life has been unfair to both of us. I know Mahi liked me a lot and even she would have wanted to stay with me forever. But, destiny had written something else for us. My life is shattered now and I don't know how I will survive without Mahi. I want you to allow me to marry Mahi before her cremation. I know it sounds weird and foolish but I don't want to regret my entire life", said Ravi with tears in his eyes.

Anandita and Abhimanyu were surprised to hear this.

"What are you saying Ravi? This can't happen!", said Abhimanyu while clearing his throat.

"I know uncle you might be thinking I have gone crazy. But I'm speaking with full consciousness. Though not sanctioned by law, posthumous marriages are still held in different parts of India. Several communities in Kerala's Kasaragod district especially in villages continue to practice a custom called *'Pretha Kalyanam'*. I want to follow that tradition and marry Mahi", pleaded Ravi.

Anandita and Abhimanyu looked at each other. They knew people would mock them for performing the unusual rituals. Both of them desired to see Mahi's wedding but Ravi's idea surprised them. They were unable to speak anything. They were already broken. They had lost their adorable daughter and people's opinion would hardly matter to them now. Ravi pleaded to them a lot and finally they agreed to perform this uncommon ritual.

Ravi bought a small box filled with *sindoor* (vermilion) and applied it on Mahi's forehead. Anandita cried while seeing this. Ravi's eyes were moist and he smiled at Mahi. Abhimanyu watched him from a distance and tried to stop crying.

"I will keep you in my heart forever Mahi. I promise. I love you unconditionally", said Ravi while sitting beside Mahi's body.

After some time, Anandita and Abhimanyu's relatives and friends reached their home to mourn the death of their beloved daughter.

The grief stricken parents and Ravi then started preparation for cremation of Mahi.

30

Anandita couldn't forget the dreadful night in the hospital and the hours of silence that engulfed the drawing room where their relatives had gathered. She couldn't believe that Mahi was no longer with them. She felt desolated. The only hope and happiness in Anandita and Abhimanyu's life vanished within a second.

The day to bid final goodbye to Mahi had come. Mahi's body was preserved in a stainless steel freezer box covered with a glass sheet bought from a local Gurudwara at Indore. Anandita cried incessantly. Ravi's eyes were fixed on Mahi's body. He stared at her with tears in his eyes.

"My baby is looking so beautiful", whispered Ravi and tears rolled down from his eyes.

Hindu as believers of reincarnation believe that it's only their body that dies. The soul is reborn in a different form after death. This recycling of life continues until the soul finds its true nature.

Mahi's body was given a bath by Anandita and female family members as ordered by the chief priest of their family. Many Hindu families recognize the importance of the bath to prepare the body for the cremation. Mahi was dressed in a bridal red saree with make up.

"My bride is the most beautiful bride in the whole universe", Ravi whispered again.

Mahi's body was kept in the drawing room with her head facing southward. The body was displayed in a simple, inexpensive Casket with sandalwood paste applied on her forehead. A large garland was placed around her neck.

Anandita was inconsolable. She cried and hugged the body of her 23-years-old daughter. Thousands of people gathered at the cantonment to bid a tearful adieu to Mahi. The entire country mourned Mahi's death. Around 20,000 people from all walks of life- medical fraternity, student organizations, journalists, Femina members, friends and relatives of Abhimanyu- gathered at Mhow Cantonment to pay their last respect to Mahi. All roads leading to Mahi's home were lined up with banners in her honour. Scores of mourners thronged their house between 6 am to 9 am to catch the last glimpse of Mahi.

The residents of Mhow Cantonment and Indore sprinkled flowers on the road in the loving memory of the daughter of Indian Army when the convoy carrying the mortal remains of Mahi passed through. The Government of Madhya Pradesh also provided her state honours.

People chanted "Dr.Mahi! Miss India Amar Rahe! Bharat Mata ki Jay!"

The funeral procession began its journey at 10 am and reached the Shiv Dham crematorium at 12 noon. Several people gathered around the place. Large screens were also installed for the people who couldn't enter during cremation proceedings.

Ravi and Mahi's parents placed the wreaths on the body while trying to hold back their tears and appealed to the people to maintain peace. Ravi couldn't stop his tears and was crying uncontrollably. He lit the funeral pyre at the cremation and the last rites were performed. Mahi was cremated with full state honours at 12:30 pm. The roads were turned into flower beds from Indore to Mhow cantonment. Anandita and Abhimanyu returned home with intense shock and overwhelming sadness and despair. Ravi was lost and he believed that life had no meaning now. He decided never to marry again and took the responsibility of Mahi's parents.

OTHER BOOKS WRITTEN BY THE AUTHOR

1st - LOVE ON VENTILATOR
Ajit never felt insulted as he understood the mental agony and turmoil of Sudha. He will never leave Sudha with a broken heart and hope. He was not to satisfy his adrenaline rush as he had a firm belief that desire was a reason for mating in animals' way.

2nd - LOVE TRILOGY WHO TO COMPLAIN
She was not responding to people and surrounding activities. The doctor arrived and, after examination, termed this as COMA or COMATOSE. He advised Ajit to treat it as a medical emergency.

3rd - IT'S OK TO FALL IN LOVE AGAIN

She also knew that a single woman, both at home, college, or at work, has to face many advances from men young and old, married and unmarried.

To be single and especially an unwed mother is taken as that she is available or easy to gain access to.

4th – THE SON ROSE FROM THE WEST

Anandita told Anwar – You are a Muslim completely different than what I preach and practice. I understand that your marriage laws are different from ours, so our alliance and resonance will need to be defined by you well before we take a plunge.

5th – MOHINI THE TIGRESS

Mohini was considered second-degree manslaughter, but Kuldeep always knew that there had to be a reason for her action. She was not born criminal from her mother's womb. He would marry her no matter what the consequences would be.

6th – LOVE LOST IN TRANSIT

"Everyone has a right to live life on his or her terms, so why not Sandra?" She thought to herself. Just because she was a divorcee, it didn't mean that her sex life had to dry. Sandra was young and had her bodily needs, so she was sometimes finding her life entering the second phase of her sexual life.

7th – INDU THE PARCHED WOMAN

Ajay was restless, wondering how he would react when Pihu would touch him. The bedroom smell divine, like rose petals, were sprinkled everywhere. It was extremely romantic, and the fragrance of Pihu ignited his senses. They could see the view of half city and full moon over the Arabian Sea.

8th – MOTHER VS SURROGATE (A TALE OF TWO MOTHERS)

Monika would never take the initiative like any western or high profile girl to propose to Ravindra even if she liked him. She would want Ravindra to do something crazy to win her over though she always loved a bit of fantasy of being chased.

9th – IS THAT LOVE OR FANTASY?

Afreen was like a child, innocent but bonded with big dark eyes under some fear. Sometimes in those moments in the dining room, Manzoor would prolong the conversation, which implied that he wanted to sleep with Afreen. Afreen usually used to get nervous, but a mental strength was developed beneath Afreen's physical fragility. She used to leave him, got food for herself, and went to another room and bolted it from inside as she was always scared because she was a tiny sophisticated female and Manzoor this big tall guy.

10th – LOVE WILL THAT CHERISH OR PERISH?

Her brain was still deep in mourning, but other parts of Amy were in overdrive, reminding her that she was still alive, healthy, and up for fun. Casually when Amy discussed this state of her mind and body to one of her very close friends of college-era, she suggested this to be normal and good for her in getting back on the horse. The same friend also commented that our sexuality is a gift of God to be proud of. "She agreed that despite being raised conservatively by a father in the Church, we could not challenge the physical design of God."

11th – RUKHSAAR, THE WOMAN OF SUBSTANCE

Frankly speaking, I have not come to rebuild my relationship but remove the guilt from my mind and soul, for I have hurt you and your family. I can't live with this guilt for my lifetime. This guilt is becoming an unrelenting source of pain, and this kind of guilt is insidious and self-destructive.

12th – URMILA-UNSPOKEN & UNAPPRECIATED

One day, I will walk alone to the Sharyu. I shall light a pyre all by myself. When Sita wanted a pyre, you made it for her, but I will have to do it myself in my case. I will do that. Sita entered the pyre to prove her purity, but I don't have to prove anything to anybody. I will not come out of the fire unscathed. I want to annihilate myself. That night will be my last night of loneliness, rejection, abandonment, and longing.

13th – RAGHU, THE SELFMADE MAN

During summers, we used to sleep in an open sky area. One day I noticed that I was covered by the bed sheet to avoid cold and dew, and the eldest daughter did it. Afterward, it became my habit of not covering myself, hoping that she would do it. It was done so long as I continued sleeping in the open.

14th – YE HOSLA KAISE RUKE

Life won't stop for you. Life can not stop for anyone. If it did we would never get anywhere. Instead of grieving and loving one man (Abhimanyu), Love the whole world.

15th – VIDUR (Archer, Strategist & Mahatma)
Vidur was an archer better than Arjun. He was a strategist for both Dhritarashtra and Yudhistar. He was the biggest devotee of Lord Krishna. He died as Mahatma. His Rajdharma did not allow him to fight. His Vidur Neeti is a guiding force even today.

16th – LOVE FROM THE OTHER WORLD
Abhimanyu was an army brat. After his engineering graduation he joined Google. He married Divya Singh, his IITD college mate. They had a son Parikshit. During Abhimanyu's vacations he went for mountain expedition at Mountain Kamet but never returned. Divya upon insistence of her parents and in-laws married her colleague Ranveer Singh. What happens hereafter…